T0285081

Please visit our website, www.west44books.com.
For a free color catalog of all our high-quality books,
call toll free 1-800-398-2504.

Cataloging-in-Publication Data
Names: Karyus Quinn, Kate.
Title: Always June / Kate Karyus Quinn.
Description: New York : West 44, 2023. | Series: West 44 YA verse
Identifiers: ISBN 9781978596382 (pbk.) | ISBN 9781978596375
(library bound) | ISBN 9781978596399 (ebook)
Subjects: LCSH: Children's poetry, American. | Children's poetry,
English. | English poetry.
Classification: LCC PS586.3 K39 2023 | DDC 811'.60809282--dc23

First Edition

Published in 2023 by
Enslow Publishing LLC
2544 Clinton Street
Buffalo, NY 14224

Editor: Caitie McAneney
Designer: Katelyn E. Reynolds

Photo Credits: Cvr VectorPot/Shutterstock.com.

Printed in the United States of America

CPSIA compliance information: Batch #CW23W44: For further information contact
Enslow Publishing LLC at 1-800-398-2504.

"I wonder what it would be like to live in a world where it was always June."
— L. M. Montgomery, *Anne of the Island.*

# THE TRUTH

will set
you
FREE.

That's what
they say.
Like
FREE
is the
best thing
anyone
can be.

Like
maybe
I should
THANK
my sister's
ex-boyfriend
Er-*ick*
for taking
a video
of me
puking
into my
kitchen
sink.
Like he
did me a

favor
showing
it to the
whole
     darn
        school.

Did
Er-*ick*
set me
FREE?

Cause
I don't
*feel*
FREE.

To be
totally
honest,
this truth
that Er-*ick*
let loose
feels like
a trap
worse
than
the lie          *(I'm not hungry)*
that
lined
my
old
cage.

# THE DIFFERENCE THOUGH IS THIS

A lie
can be
uncovered
or confessed.

But truth
is
                forever.

Or at
least
until
I graduate.

                The truth hurts.

That's another
thing
they say.

That one—
                I believe.

# I'D BEEN INVISIBLE

A wallpaper
type of
girl.

No one
noticed
me.

I liked it
that way.

Mostly.

Then …

                    the video.

One
47.3-
second
clip.

Me
with my
finger
down my
throat,
my face
stretched
and
ugly

as I
viciously
vomited.

The whole
school
has seen it.

In the last
two months,

the whole WORLD
has seen it.
   (Thanks a lot, internet!)
And they
will
        NOT
let me
forget
it.

# now

I am
KNOWN.

Kids
call me
Scarf and Barf.
Or sometimes
just
Barf.

One boy
barks it
at me
like a
confused
dog.

*BARF! BARF!*

Another time,
        a girl
                pointed
            right
    at me.

Said,

*That's her?*
*But …*
    *I don't get it.*

*She's*
    not
        *skinny.*

I tuck my
chin(s)
and pretend
not to hear
and pretend
not to see
and pretend
that none
of this
bothers me.

# KEEP YOUR HEAD HELD HIGH!

That's what
my older sister
Mae said
after my
secrets
became
       a joke.

And the
punch line
was
always
       me.

*Don't let*
*them*
*get to*
*you,*

she said.

*Who cares*
     *what*
      *those*
        *idiots*
         *think?*

I do.

I care.

# I DONT KNOW HOW NOT TO

I am not like Mae.

She has
always
been
certain
and sure.

She is
who
she is.

Her pretty,
homemade,
old-fashioned
dresses
made to fit her
proudly plus-size
figure.

The kitten
heels and
curled hair.

She created
the world
she wanted
to live in.

A world
where she
never diets.

A world
where she
posts on
social media
a pic
of herself
taste testing
her latest
batch of
brownies
and somehow
ignores
the nasty
comments.

A world
where she's
*NEVER*
anyone
other than
herself.

Wherever
she goes
she is
   Always
    Mae.

# I ENVY THAT

Even now,
when everyone knows
my worst secret,
I don't feel
FREE

to be

           always

               *me* ...

                      whoever

                         *that*

                           might be.

## SOMEHOW

there's
    TOO MUCH
of me
… but also
       not enough.

I wonder
what it's like
to live
in my body
without wishing
that I'm
    anybody
      other
        than

                me.

# THE SCHOOL COUNSELOR

Mr. Mann
calls me
to his office.
I'm honestly surprised
it took him *this* long.
He apologizes for the
*backlog.*
He is kind
and concerned
as he tells me,

*You're not*
*in trouble.*

(But it feels like I am.)

*However,*
*I'm very*
*concerned*
*about the*
*contents*
*of that video.*

*Eating disorders*
*are a matter*
*we take*
*seriously.*

# EATING DISORDER

I hate those
two
    stupid
        words.

It sounds like
a handwritten
sign
stuck onto a
vending machine
that's stopped
working.

**OUT OF ORDER**

At least
he didn't
use words
like

        aNOreXia
          or
           BuLiMiA.

*June,*

Mr. Mann prods.

*Tell me,*
*is this a*
*regular thing?*

# I TRY TO DISAPPEAR

into the
battered
old chair.  (Lately I'm always trying to disappear.)

Trying to forget
how I told
Mae
     I'd do better.
           I'd fix this.

                          Fix myself.

Which is
great
       … in theory.

In reality,
though …
     I can
        barely
            eat
       in front
    of others
  these days.

It feels like
everyone's
watching
      each bite

counting
        each chew
noting
        each swallow.

Why can't we eat privately?
Like how we pee?
        ///In separate stalls///
        ///divided///
        ///ignoring///
        ///the bodies///
        ///on either side///
        ///of us.///

Wouldn't that be nice?

To never again
watch someone
else moving
wet mushy food
around inside
their mouths?

Or maybe
that's just
        me.

## LOOK,

Mr. Mann
says into
the silence.

*We have a
school psychologist
who comes
once a week—
if you need help,
we'll squeeze
you in.*

SQUEEZE me in.

Where I don't

                                      fit.

Again,
taking up
too
  much       SPACE.

No thank you.
I can do this alone.

Since
the Homecoming Dance,
I haven't
puked.

Since
the Homecoming Dance,
I've eaten
       ... most
              meals.

Since
the Homecoming Dance,
I've gained
ten pounds.

It's probably
mostly
water weight.        (I hope it's mostly water weight.)

I don't need the
school psychologist.

I'm not going to
waste her time.

It's just food.
It's just eating.
It's just self-control.

I can do this.

I've got this.

I just have to
             try
                  harder.

# FIGHTING

every day
to be better
to do better.

Winter is
all about
willpower
while the
blurrrrrr
of gray days
keep whirling by.
Nothing good
in them
except
when one
ends.

Mae is busy
applying to
colleges
while I
focus on
avoiding
ALL
holiday cookies.
I
only gain
five pounds
over the break.

Mom is busy
with her new boyfriend
Bill,
who she spends
every second with.

Back at school,
my best friend
Lacey meets a boy
on stage crew
and now is
in love
and with him
all the time.

Leaving me
                    alone.

And I'm trying
not to notice
all the
GET IN SHAPE FOR THE NEW YEAR
things
all over the place.
I keep trying to eat normally ...
whatever that even means.

I dump the leftover
Christmas candy
into the trash.

I DON'T
let myself

20

think of the
leftover
Valentine's heart
full of
fancy caramels
Mom's new boyfriend
gave her.

And I
pretend
not to see
Toby—

                                    Toby who
                                        once
                                    kissed me.
                                    Toby who
                                      is a boy
                                  with secrets
                                         and I
                                      was one
                                      of them.

—while he
pretends
not to see
me,
even when
we're both
walking down
the same street
in the same
direction
on our way home.

## WINTER BOOTS

change to
sneakers
as trees bud
and the
school year
is nearly
done.

And my jeans
from last year
are too tight,
and I know
it's all the
jelly beans
in my
jelly belly,
so I cut
out sugar—
           just sugar—
because
everyone
knows it's
bad
anyway.
And drink
green tea
to help with the
water weight.

This is
healthy.
And I
have NOT
puked.

So, I'm better now.

The dance
was months
ago.
Everything
has changed
since then.

I've changed.

I'm now just a
normal girl
who doesn't eat
                    sugar, fat, dairy, or carbs,
            fasts on
    Wednesday and Saturday,
            drinks 30 ounces
                a day
                    of pure green tea
        with a slice of lemon,
                and prefers
fruit and veggie smoothies
                    as meal replacements.

## WHEN MAE GETS

her college acceptance
letter,
            we celebrate.

Her dream
is coming
true.

New York City.
Fashion School.

She is getting
away.
She is getting
out.

When Mae gets
her acceptance
letter,
            I cry.

Secretly.

Alone.

At night
in my bed
into my pillow
to conceal
the sound.

I am
losing
the
one
person
I can
count on.

When Mae
makes
a cake
to celebrate,
I eat
a slice
and
pretend
it is
                    *fine*
and
that I'm
definitely

                    *not*
calculating
calories
from all the
          butter
and
          sugar
and
          heavy cream.

# LATER,

even after
brushing
my teeth
twice,
I can
still taste
the slick
sweetness
on my
tongue.

It
makes
me
sick.

It
makes
 me
hungry.

Everyone is
asleep
as I creep
down
    the
       stairs.

The cake
is on the
pretty pedestal
Mae
got
for
Christmas.

I grab a fork,
lift an edge
of the
plastic wrap
and

**stab.**

One bite.

Just
    one
        bite.

It's so

small

it doesn't
even
leave
a dent.

I lick
    the
        fork
            clean.

One bite.

That's
what
I
promised
myself.

One bite
      wasn't
        so bad.

    One bite
      wasn't
        enough.

Just
      one more
          one bite
              more
                 one bite

more
  one bite
       more
          one bite
               more
                one bite
   more
     one bite
       more
         one bite
           more
            one bite—

There's
     no
more.

The plate is empty.

My stomach is full.

I don't                    I don't
want                       plan
to be                      to be
sick.                      sick.

It just
        happens.

All the
cake
comes
back       up
         up
      ᵈᵘ
      up.

I brush
my teeth
once more.

And then
I wash the
                  pretty pedestal platter,
                       put it away,
                         and go
                         to bed.

29

# THE NEXT DAY

I wait.

Sick, hating myself.
Knowing Mae
must hate me,
too.

But Mae
never says
a thing.

# BILL WASN'T JUST ANOTHER GUY

We knew it was serious
with Bill when Mom
started going out every
Friday night,
squeezing into her
tummy-tucker,
butt-lifter
jeans.

*What?*

she demanded
when she caught
Mae and I
exchanging glances.

*You want me*
*to die alone?*

We didn't.
And Bill seemed                    … okay.

But it turns out
Bill was                                  married.

Mom found this out just last week.

He told her
as he bit into the
grilled cheese

he'd just
made himself—

*My wife doesn't let me
eat dairy.
We're a vegan household.*

                                        *YOUR **WIFE**!*

And then Mom
grabbed the pan
from the stove
and Bill apparently
realized his mistake
and                                        ran.

# I GUESS THAT MOMENT WAS
# A TURNING POINT

because Bill
left his wife         (or she kicked him out).

Either way,
Bill and
ALL his things
soon FILL
our small house.

He moves in
on a Thursday afternoon
while Mae and I
are at school.

We come home
to find him
cooking dinner.

*You girls like tacos?*
he asks with a grin.

*Of course they do,*
Mom answers for us
while shooting us
THE LOOK
that tells us
to keep our mouths
         SHUT.

So we do.
And the
only response
I'm allowed
is to
**StOmP**
upstairs
and then

# SLAM SHUT

my bedroom
door.

# ONE MORE PERSON

doesn't seem
like much.

But Bill takes up
A LOT of room.

First off,
he works
odd hours,
depending on
his shifts
at the plant.

It means he's
always around
when you *don't*
want him to be.

And it
doesn't matter
that he's trying
so hard
to fit in
and be extra helpful:
getting groceries,
making dinner,
doing the dishes,
even asking if
he can make me a
brown-bag lunch.

# TRUTH IS

Bill might be
the nicest guy
Mom's ever dated.

But all the
meals he cooks
fills our house
with new smells—
making it foreign.

And he stuffs
the fridge
with cheese
while
ice cream
overflows
the freezer.

For him,
he's making up
lost time
from all those
vegan years.

For me,
though,
it's a temptation
too hard
to resist.

# PLUS HE HAS THIS HABIT

of taking off
his socks
wherever
and whenever.
Then just leaving
them lying on the
couch
    or floor
        or kitchen chair.

*Sorry, sorry!*

he says
when I find one
and pick it up
between two fingers.

Taking it,
he stuffs it
in a pocket.
*Bad habit.*
*I got hot and cold feet.*
*Always taking my socks*
*on and off,*
*then on again.*

He's embarrassed
and I should
tell him
it's okay.

But I am a new June.
A tough June.
A June pushed to her limits
and uninterested
in making friends.

And this June
says to Bill,

*Well, they smell.*

And then walks away
before he can reply.

# PACKING

Sorting.
Boxing.
Giving stuff away.

Mae prepares
for college
like she is leaving

                         forever.

Tidying up
ALL
the loose ends.                 (including me)


In a week, she will graduate.

She goes to grab more boxes,
leaves her phone out on her bed
unlocked.

I grab it, laughing,
planning to take
a funny selfie
for Mae to find later.

But the phone opens to Mae's chat
with her new college friends.

She always makes friends
so easily.

Already they are
besties.

And I see *my* name.

June binged again yesterday

I stare at the those words
                in black and white.

    And          I         can't        breathe.

1. You don't talk about it.

2. You don't name it.

3. You pretend not to know.


Those are the rules.

And Mae broke them.

                        Mae broke us.

# I KEEP READING

her friends' replies
with poison
in my veins.

They feel sorry for her
for having to deal
                    with me.

Oh that must be so hard!

                    She needs help.

                    You should say something.

I want to write back,

        YOU DON'T KNOW US—NOT REALLY!

But instead,
        I just stop eating.

# COLD SHOULDER AND NO LUNCH FOR A WEEK

And then Mae says,

*June, we gotta talk
about your eating.*

I give her the same hard look
that I have perfected
on Bill.

I shoot back,
*Maybe we should talk
about* YOUR *eating,
You're too* FAT
*to gain
the freshman fifteen.*

I have never
      called Mae
            FAT.

It's a word
      we *never* use.

But she broke
      the rules
            first.

So I say this
awful thing
even though
the words
in my mouth
taste like
the worst
kind of bile.

I hate them.

I hate myself.

But I don't say I'm sorry.

And I don't take it back.

# IT DOESN'T END THERE

Mom doesn't like
              to be told.
Mom can't be
              pushed.
Mom must be
              nudged.

      Slowly.                             Cautiously.

But Mae is determined
to make my eating
                  a thing.

She finds Mom in the kitchen. Says,

*June isn't*
       *just dieting.*
*She's binging*
       *and purging.*
*She's skipping meals.*

      *She's*
         *sick.*

Mae says all of this
in front of me, Mom,
and also
             Bill.

I am so mad.

I can't even speak.
So Bill talks first.
Of all people.                    BILL!

*I don't wanna*
*butt in,*
*but that does*
*sound serious.*

Then Mom
comes to my rescue.

She tells Bill
he doesn't know
what he's talking about.

Then she turns
to me.
*June, are you sick?*

I shake my head. No.
Not hesitating.
Not caring
about truth or lies.

I am too mad
at Mae
for picking at this
*now* when
I've tried so hard
all year.

All the
sacrifices
I made to seem
better, perfect, fine.
All Mae sees
are the slipups.

*No,*
I say again.

*Are you kidding—?*
Mae starts.

Mom holds up
a hand, stopping her.
*That's enough,*
Mom says in her
do-not-make-me-lose-my-temper
voice.

But Mae is past caring.

*June needs help.*
*Therapy.*
*Can't you see?*
*She doesn't know*
        *how to stop.*

Mom slams her hands
on the table.
*I don't see anything.*

Mae doesn't even flinch.

*No, because you're*
*too busy*
*looking the other way*
*while June*
          *kills herself.*

# SLAP!

Mom's hand
meets Mae's cheek.

Hard and fast.

We all freeze
for a moment,

                    shocked.

Even Mom.

Then Bill grabs Mom.

Mae runs to her room.

And I head
straight for
the bathroom
to throw up
everything
I've ever eaten.

## THE FIGHT

means an icy June.
It means that Mae
leaves in July
          instead
                    of August.
She decides to rent a place
with friends
and get a head start
on job hunting in the city.

The Fight
means that Mae
          looks at me
                    and says,
*I need to get away.*
          *If you decide—*
                    *if you need—*
                              ***when*** *you get help,*
                                        *call me.*
*But otherwise,*
          *I need a break.*

The Fight
is how I lose my sister.
My ally.

My one true
friend.

# I CAN'T FORGIVE

Mae
for leaving.

Or for
everything
she said.

I hold onto
my anger.

I feed it
scraps
to keep
it alive.

Like Bill.

He now
watches me
all the time,
but especially

               when I eat.

Or don't eat.

And I
notice him
keeping track
of what's
in the cupboards.

When a bag of chips
disappears,
he says,

*Hey June,*
*it's not a problem*
*but I noticed*
*the chips are gone ...*

He acts
all pretend-casual,
but beneath that,
I can
feel
his tension.

So I lie.

I tell him that
I have no idea
what
     he's
        talking
            about.

He doesn't believe me.

I can tell.

Even though he nods
and says,

*Yeah, okay, sure.*

# THIS IS MAE'S FAULT

What I eat
shouldn't be
Bill's business.

And I hear him
talking with Mom.

*Well, maybe she*
            *does need help?*
he says, hesitant.

*Oh, gimme a break,*
Mom says.
*I was always worrying*
*over my weight*
*at that age, too.*

She brushes him off
                        so easily.
Then switches the
conversation
to something else.

Later,
when I tell her
that Bill's
all up in my grill
every time I
enter the kitchen,
I expect her to take

my side.
Instead, she snaps.

*You're weird about food,*
*June.*
**Everyone**
        *in this house*
                *knows it.*
*Eat normal.*
*Stop splashing puke*
*all over the porcelain.*
*Then maybe Bill*
*and everyone else*
*will get off your case.*

I am stunned.
Mom's never minded my …
                                dieting.
That's what she's always called it.

But Mae,
and now Bill,
put it in her head
that I'm broken.

OUT OF ORDER

That I'm a problem.

I don't tell her
that I'm trying to
do better.

That I'm not
binging.    (as much)

52

That I'm
　　　eating …
　　　　　　maybe not normal.
　　　　　　　　　　But more.

Enough so that
my stomach doesn't
feel like a
constant ache
inside of me.

I can't tell her
because the words
are all
　　　　　　knotted up
inside of me …

Along with
the fear
that maybe
　　　　*trying*
isn't enough.

I'm starting
to think
that maybe
I don't even know
how to be　　　　　　　　　how to eat

　　　　normal.

Not anymore.

53

# I HIDE IN MY ROOM

for all of July,
cause it's the only place
Bill won't go.

Mae doesn't text (fat chance).
Lacey doesn't text (not anymore).
Toby doesn't text (obviously).

I'm left alone.
But in August,
it's too hot
with AC only downstairs.

My fan does nothing
but stir
the same sticky air.

I escape outside
and start walking
with no destination
in mind.

Just away.

But then,
        at the end of the block,
there it is.

Like an old friend
I'd forgotten.

# TEN PIN ALLEY

Normally,
I don't go
this way.

School is the other way.
*Everything* is the other way.

This is the
not-so-nice
part of town.

A pawn shop
sits next to Ten Pin.

There are bars
on the windows.

When I was
a kid,
my dad brought
me and Mae here.

He drank at the bar
while we bowled.

As long as we all walked,
Mom didn't mind.

Or she didn't
until the day
we came running

into the house
panicked,
wanting our
little red wagon
so we could get Dad
off the sidewalk—
                    where he'd fallen—
                              and bring him home.

That was the
beginning
of the end,
I guess.

Soon after,
he moved South
and we never
saw him again.

There were some
birthday cards
and phone calls …
for a while.

But then they
tapered off
into silence.

Now
cold air
and old memories
wrap
around me
the moment

I open
the door.

Everything is
the same in Ten Pin.

The smell.
The lights.
The long, dark bar.
And the lanes
all lit up like a party.

It's not like
my dad
was so great
or like he left
a big hole
in my life.

But just the same …
being here
makes me feel
weirdly closer
to him.

# AND MAE, TOO

She was my partner in crime here,
chasing balls down the lane.

We invented bumper ball,
speed ball,
and all sorts of other
new ways to bowl.

And I wasn't too bad at it.

Without thinking,
I pull crumpled bills
from my pocket
and hand them over
for shoes
and a lane.

# GUTTER BALL

Once.
Twice.
Three times.

Apparently,
bowling is not
just like
riding a bike.

I'm ready to quit
when—

*You're turning your wrist.*

It's a girl
in the lane beside mine.

I recognize her
from school—Ricki.
Blue hair frames
the hearing aids
behind
each of her ears.

She's famously loud
and opinionated.
The type of person
who once put together
a protest
over girls not being

allowed to wear shirts
with spaghetti straps.

We've never spoken before.

Now,
without waiting
for a response,
she comes over,
grabs hold of my wrist,
and guides my arm
through the motion of
throwing the ball.

*Here,*

she says,
pausing the motion
with my arm
stretched out
in front of me.

Tapping my wrist,
she then rotates it,
just slightly.

*There. Like that.*
*Feel the difference?*

She steps away,
but I leave my arm
where she's placed it.

*I think so?*
I say, more because it's
what she wants to hear.

She nods.
*Good. Try it again.*

I should probably
tell her
to get lost
and leave me

alone.

But I've been alone
for what feels like
forever.

                                    I'm sick of alone.

Grabbing my ball,
I approach the lane
and think of
my wrist
and how it felt
when she
turned it.

I pull my arm back
and send the ball
toward the pins.

This time
it stays straight
            and true.

Six pins fall.
A seventh wobbles,
considering,
before tumbling, too.

*Nice!*
Ricki is right next to me,
pointing to
the remaining pins.

*There,*
she says.
*That's where you*
*want to aim the ball*
*to get the spare.*

Again, I do what
she tells me.
And again,
it works
as if she's
taken control
of my limbs.

It almost feels
            like magic.

## FOR A MOMENT

I wish
that I could
turn
my whole life
over
to her.

      Eat this, not that.

      No, don't think about
                the fat.

      Okay, that's enough.
                Stop or you'll be sick.

I can't control
my body,
    but maybe
    she can.

As if reading
my mind,
she says,

*That settles it.*
*You're joining*
*the bowling team.*

It's an announcement.
Not a question.

63

Like what I think
about it
        doesn't even matter.

And I realize
that actually
      *I do*
want a say
in my own life.

*No, thanks,*
I tell her.

But this girl
is not the type
to take
      no
for an answer.

*You're a junior, right?*
She sticks out a hand.
*Me too.*
*I'm Ricki.*

As if I don't know her name.
Everyone does.

After a moment
of hesitation,
I take her hand in mine.

*June,*
I say.

She nods.
*I know.*
*You're Mae's sister.*
*I interviewed her*
*for the school paper*
*last spring.*

I remember this.

It's not a good memory.

## MAE GETTING INTO

the New York City
art school
was a BIG deal.

The paper put
her interview
on the front page
along with
her senior picture
where she looked
gorgeous.

Like an old-fashioned,
plus-size
pinup model.

The paper comes out
monthly, and then sits piled in
the cafeteria, library, and front office.

Mostly I forget it exists.

But Mae's month,
I saw it
                    everywhere.

On a back table
in the library
with bubble words
over Mae's head

reading,
                    "I'm too fat to
                              wear normal clothes."

Crumpled in the hallway
near my locker.
Someone had taken
a red pen and
circled then labeled
all the places
where Mae
needs improvement.

Upper arms.          FAT
Legs.                FAT
Belly.               FAT
Chin and cheeks.     FAT
Cankles.             FAT

They circled ALL of her.

I tore up the ones I found.
But I'm sure there were more.

I'm sure Mae saw them.
But she never said a thing.

A part of me
              was mad at her.

Furious she put
herself out there
for kids to draw

on her face.
And then
for pretending
to not
care.

But mostly
I hated her
for being fat
and not
knowing
        enough
            to be ashamed.

## SPEAKING OF COLLEGE...

Ricki's words
jolt me
back to the present
and I realize
I missed
half of what
she said.

Luckily, she keeps
talking and I
piece things together.

*You know colleges
like to see
extracurricular activities
on your application.
Plus—*

Before she can
say more,
four girls
near the entrance
yell out,
*Ricki!*

She spins to face them,
a grin on her lips.

*Guys! I got a live one!*
she hollers back.

They join us
and I recognize
them all from school.

Tall and dark-skinned,
her hair in a curly
bun on top of her head,
Ammiah Smith
throws an arm
around Ricki's shoulders.

She tells me,
*If she offered you money*
*to join the team—*
                              *that's illegal.*
Then adds,
*Also, she doesn't*
                    *have it.*

Ricki laughs at this.
*This is Striker.*
*She's our star.*

Ammiah shrugs off
this praise.
*Or you can call me*
                      *Ammiah*
*just like my mom does.*

She pauses, then adds,
*You're June, right?*
*We had ELA together*
*last year.*

I nod.
*Yeah, I remember.*

Holding my breath,
I wait for her
to say more
and mention
the video.

But instead,
she just gives Ricki
a friendly shove.

*Girl, you gotta stop
trying to recruit
every female who
comes in here
just wanting to bowl.*

Turning her attention
back to me,
she adds,
*Last week,
she made a poor
middle school kid
                    cry.*

Ricki scoffs.
*She was tall for her age!
How was I
supposed to know
she wasn't in
high school yet?*

Ammiah ignores this.

The other girls chime in.
*You wanted to poach the*
*track team's shot put girls.*

        *She tried to go*
           *after the golf team, too.*

               *Her next plan was to start*
                  *cold-calling every girl*
                     *in the school.*

Ricki throws
her hands up
even as she laughs.
*We need six people*
*for a team. And look—*

She points to me
and all their attention
comes my way.
I take a step back.
*June has potential.*
     *She takes direction,*
           *can make adjustments.*

This earns thoughtful
looks and nods.
*Plus, she seems cool.*
*She's got a good vibe.*
*I think she'd*
      *fit in with us.*

# I LOOK AT THE FIVE OF THEM

Do I fit in?

In some ways …

                                        maybe.

These don't look
like girls who play
teenagers on TV.
They aren't skinny
with perfect hair
and skin.

Ammiah looks like
a bodybuilder.

Ricki is probably
the same size
as me, but
she stands TALLER.
Legs spread
Feet planted.
Taking up space
without apology.

The other three
are similar.

They are themselves.

Gangly with oversized glasses
and a jagged bob,
Kimi started the
Asian representation club
at our school.

I vaguely know Laurel
from art class but have never really
registered her
as anything
other than a
tiny, angry emo girl.

And finally Polly
is a senior, but
she made a splash
last year
for getting a
face tatt—
a broken heart
on her
left cheekbone
to mark her
grandmother's death—
that the school
made her cover
with a Band-Aid.
Right now she's
wearing suspenders with shorts
and a rainbow Pride T-shirt.

Mae would fit in with them.
But I don't.

# THEY SEEM FEARLESS

And I am …

*Sorry,*
I mutter,
already backpedaling.
And then—
even as Ricki calls

*Wait!*—

I'm turning
my eyes
to the exit.

The automatic
doors open,
and as I step through,

I hear Ricki call,

*We'll be here*
*all week*
*if you change*
*your mind!*

# I HOLD OUT

for three days.

Once again hiding in my
sweatbox bedroom.

At dinner, Bill announces,

*If you think this is hot,*
                    *you're in for a surprise!*
*Weather reporter says*
        *this coming heat wave's*
                    *gonna break records!*

I open my window,
trying to catch
a breeze,
but instead I
see Toby.

## TOBYS BIG SECRET

was his mom.
He pretended she didn't exist
  to everyone
        except me.

But now she's
back in his life
making it
messy, ugly, and loud
as she throws his things
       out the front door
         and into the front yard.

Clothes. Books.
Underwear.
An old stuffed bear.

*This is my house,*
she yells.
*You don't tell me*
       *what to do!*

Toby grabs his things
off the lawn.
I can see
how hard he's trying
to be invisible,
to make her
and this whole
situation

          go away.

Having the
whole neighborhood
see his mother—
fresh from drug rehab—
is his nightmare
come true.

What would his basketball buddies
say if they found out?

Toby's mom jumps
on his back,
and the two of them
whirl round and round.

Toby's mom
screeches
        and claws
                and curses.

At last,
Toby shakes her off
and she hits the ground

                                        hard.

*It's Grandma's house,*
he says, just barely
loud enough
for me to hear.

Then he turns his back
            on his mother
                    as she starts to cry.

He goes back inside,
where his secrets are safe.

I turn away, too.
        Close my window.
                Lie on my bed.

I think about how lonely
he must feel,
locked away inside,
                        alone,
    guarding himself,
        holding himself

                                    apart.

And I
        finally
                make up
                    my mind.

# I TEXT MAE

even though
it's been silent
since she left.

Still, I think this news
might be something
to make her             hate me
                                      a little bit less.

Picking up my phone,
I type,

Remember
        Ten Pin Alley?
I'm gonna be there
                      a lot …
as part of the girls'
              high school
                      bowling team!

Wish me luck?

# AS I ENTER

the bowling alley,
my phone finally
    **dings**
with Mae's reply—

> Of course I remember
>     Ten Pin.
>             We grew up there.
>
> And I'm
> **always**
> wishing you
> **all** the luck.

My throat grows
                    tight
as I read Mae's words.

Quickly,
before I can think twice,
I type back,

> Thanks!
> I miss you.
> Hope you're doing well.

Three little dots …

Then nothing.

# *YOU CAME BACK!*

Ricki cries out.

I glance up in time
to see her running toward me.
Arms outstretched.
Barely giving me
      time to brace
            for a huge
                  bear hug
                      so tight
                          that I worry
                              my ribs
                                  might crack.

The other girls
appear and
peel Ricki
off me.

*Remember our talk*
*the other day*
*about not scaring*
*people away?*
Ammiah asks.

Ricki just laughs.
*I know, I know.*
*I have no chill*
*and I need to*
*dial it down.*

She mimes turning
a knob.

*But, on the other hand …*

Ricki grins and then
throws her arms out
in my direction
like she's
displaying an
amazing prize.

*June came back!*

I expect one of them
to point out
I'm nothing
to get this excited about.
But instead
they just
smile and
say hello.

And just like that—
                without any
                    tryouts
                    or interviews
                            or tests—

I'm part of the
girls' bowling team.

# I'M ON THE TEAM

but not
    IN it.

Not like the rest of them are.

The five of them
clearly share
        stories,
           memories,
              and even nicknames.

Ricki is
        DUCK!
because
of how
many times
the ball
has slipped
from her
hands
and flown
backwards.

Ammiah is
        Striker—
for obvious
reasons.

Kimi is
        Bam Bam

because of
how she
throws
the ball,
launching it
up into the air
so that it hits
the lane
with a bang
and then
bounces
and bangs
again.

Laurel is
        RAWR
for the noise
she makes
as she
watches her
ball take
down the pins.

If it's a good one,
she's pumps her
fist and cheers
        *RAWR!*

If the ball rolls
into the gutter,
then it's a sad
mournful
        *raaawrr.*

And finally,
Polly is
    The Lobster.
I don't even
know why.

It's another
inside joke
that I'm
outside of.

# I QUICKLY LEARN

the bowling team
is more than
just bowling.

The girls are friends,
but more than that, they're—

            RADICAL FEMINIST WARRIORS.

That's Ricki's term, anyway.
And Ricki mostly run things.
And everyone else mostly lets her,
           only pulling her back
               when she gets carried away.

The others warn me
that Ricki will
run my life
if I let her.

Ammiah calls her
*a bully,*
*but one with the*
*best intentions.*

# FOR EXAMPLE

The other girls tell me how
Ricki has roped
everyone on the team
into writing op-eds
for the school newspaper.

*Soon, she'll*
*start badgering you*
*to do it, too,*
Polly predicts,
          and the others agree.

They laugh about how
last year
Ammiah's
article started a
HUGE controversy.

She wrote that
bowling was
the BEST sport
humans had
EVER come up with.
And that NO ONE
played it BETTER
than GIRLS.

Laughing,
Ammiah admitted,

*I didn't even*
*know anyone*
*read the paper*
*until people*
*started*
*yelling at me*
*in the halls.*

The idea of this
freaks me out
on her behalf.

But Ammiah
thinks it's hilarious.

And Ricki
almost glows
when remembering
the hate mail
they got.

*We made people*
*feel something.*
*We made them respond.*
*We woke them*
*from their slumber.*

# I DON'T TELL RICKI

that I'd rather let people
sleep on and leave me
                alone.

Or that my
greatest dream
is to become
so small
that I eventually
disappear
entirely.

# BREAKING THE ICE

Mae and I
are talking—
well, texting—
again. A little.

And it feels
like I can
get enough
air into
my lungs
for the
first time
in forever.

She tells me
she's found
a place
to live
and how
she has
5,000
roommates.

Three are
human,
the rest are
            cockroaches.

But
the thing

she really hates
is not having
a working oven
for baking.

At the end
of one
texting session,
she slips in
almost shyly,

I've sorta met someone.

I respond with
a row of hearts
and then ask—

A romantic someone?

There's a
long pause.

I watch
    …
        the dots
            …
                on the screen
                    …
                        as Mae
                    …
                        decides
                    …
                            what to say.

# FINALLY

Yes. I think so.

Then she adds,

Gotta go
meet some friends!

… and she's gone.

Off to her
other life
totally separate
                from me.

# ONE DAY AFTER PRACTICE

I get a text from Mae—

> How are the
> bowling girls
> today?!

I tell her about Ricki.
Joke about the whole
op-ed bully thing.

Mae responds with
a laughing emoji
and then a moment
after that—

> So, what will
> YOU
> write?

# I MUST HAVE MISLED MAE

Let her think that
I've changed just because
I joined the bowling team.

Which is sort of
what I wanted her to think.
Because she doesn't want
an ugly mess
for a sister.

But that mess is still who I am.
So I change the subject. Except…
neither of us
mentions the
awful things I said
before she left …
        which means
            I can't apologize
                  for them.

And even though
I tell Mae
every time
how much I
miss her—
    she never,
        not once,
            replies
      that she
         misses me,
            too.

# DREAMS ABOUT BOWLING

creep into my sleep.

My Spanish teacher
says that a
language remains
foreign
until you
begin to
                    dream
in it.

Maybe this
        is similar.

Or maybe
I'm just
at the
alley too often.

We practice every
single day.

I start to marvel at the little ways
my body is working
*for* me.

Planting my strong legs,
swinging my strong arm.
Landing that strike.

## RICKI SAYS

we could be
*contenders.*
She pushes us
to get better
and practice
harder.

Sometimes
my fingers hurt
from gripping
the ball.

But mostly
I don't mind.

It gets me
            out
of the house.

And also,
the girls
are fun.

Also …
        there's Benny.

# BENNY IS

Ammiah's twin brother.

He comes by
to pick her up
because—
as he loves
reminding her—
*he* has his
 driver's license
 and *she*
 does not.

To my surprise,
fearless Ammiah
is terrified
of driving.
Or as she puts it,
*What's wrong*
*with riding*
*a bike?*

When Benny's
around,
we end up
 next to
 each other.

Maybe because
we're the two
who talk
the least.

Even when
he's razzing
his sister,
he speaks
in a low
rumble.

Ricki teases him
like she's
his sister, too.

*Oy! Benny!*
*Can I give you*
*some of my*
*volume?*

She makes a big deal
out of turning up
her hearing aid.

# BENNY AND I

          sort of
know
one another.

We were
partners
in bio lab
last year.

But we
never really
talked.

Except,
that one time
after the video      (yes, *that* one)
came out.
He said to me,
out of the blue,

*Lots of idiots*
    *at this school.*

I'd tensed,
unsure if
he meant
*I* was the idiot.

But then
I saw the
look on his face.

It wasn't
the cruel sneer
or dead eyes
I'd come to
know from
other classmates.
Instead, he seemed
                    nervous.
Like he knew
he'd overstepped.

Like he cared
what I thought.

I could tell
he was
            blushing
beneath his
dark skin.

*Yeah,*
I'd agreed,
softly.
*But not*
        *everyone.*

Then we went
back to
discussing
the parts
of an
earthworm.

# THINKING BACK

I can't help
    wondering …

Did Benny like me then?
Because I sorta
    think that I
        like him
            now.

# A LETTER FROM SCHOOL

I have to get
a physical
for the bowling team.

The pediatrician
I've been seeing
my whole life
is an older man
with a
shiny bald head
and eyes that never
seem to
fully

        meet

my own.

As usual,
he lectures me
on my         weight.

*Your BMI*
*is a little higher*
*than **we** like*
*to see.*
He always speaks
in the "royal we."

*Let's try to*
*remember,*

*less potato chips*
*and pop.*

Translation:
Hey, fatso,
you obviously eat
junk all day and
deserve to be fat.

*Less time*
*in front of screens*
*and more moving*
*our body*
*enough to*
*break a sweat.*

Translation:
You're lazy and
deserve to be fat.

*Which means*
*don't forget that*
*deodorant.*

Translation:
Fat people
like you
smell bad.

*What do we think,*
        *June?*
                *Can we do that?*

Translation:
There's no hope
for you,
but I have to
pretend.

He doesn't
actually
call me a
        [[fat]]
          [[lazy]]
            [[ slob]]
but it's easy
to read
between [[the lines.]]

## ON LABOR DAY

Bill proposes
         to Mom.

His divorce
is official,
and now he
wants
their relationship
to be official,
too.

*Can you
believe this
dummy?*
Mom says.
*Outta one
marriage
and straight
into another!*

Her words
are harsh,
but the
big grin
on her face
makes it
clear—
       she's thrilled.

# IN SHOCK

I always
thought
Bill was
                    temporary.

But this
means
he's not going
                    anywhere.

At least
not
anytime soon.

I want to
be happy
for Mom.

But instead
I turn to Bill and
I say,
*You cheated
    on your ex-wife.
        How long
            before you
                    cheat
                    on my mom?*

Bill jerks back,

his face white.
*I didn't.*
*I mean,*
*it was …*
                    *complicated.*

Mom puts
her hand
on Bill's arm,
making it
clear where
her loyalties
lie.

*This man*
*has only*
*ever been*
*nice*
*to you, June.*

*While you*
*stomp around*
*and sigh*
*every time*
*he enters*
*the room.*

*Well, that*
        *ends*
            *NOW.*

*We're getting*
*married*
*in November.*

*You have*
*until then*
*to figure out*
*how to be*
            *happy*
*about it.*

*Understood?*

Her tone leaves
no room for
argument.

*Understood,*
I answer.

## A NEW SCHOOL YEAR

should be
fresh and clean.
Unblemished.
A blank page
like those
filling my
new notebooks.
Studies say
we forget over the summer.

Forget math.
Forget vocabulary.
Forget how to
conjugate
Spanish verbs.

I wish everyone
would forget

                     me.

Forget what
happened

                     last year.

Forget

                     the video.

But they don't.

## BILL OFFERS

to drive me
to school
in the mornings.

*I'm up anyway,*
he says.

I know
it's meant as a
peace offering.

But to me,
it's a dilemma.

Which is worse?
                Bill or the bus?

     Bill wins.
              (just barely)

As we drive up,
I see the bowling girls
gathered near
the stairs to the side entrance.

I don't know how to act
with them at school.

I pretend not
to see them.

# BUT I CAN'T AVOID

the boy
who barks
        BARF BARF
at me.

After nearly
a year,
he still thinks
this joke
is
        HILARIOUS.

And without Mae
at my side,
he's bolder, too.
Getting up in
my face
when I don't
respond—

  *Hey, you.*
    *Can't you hear?*
    *BARF! BARF!*

I take a step back
but there's a
crowd gathering,
pressing in,
wanting a show.

Tears prick
at my eyes
but I won't
let them fall.

I hunch my
shoulders,
knowing the
bell will
ring soon
and everyone
will have to
leave me

                                    alone.

I just have to
hold out
            until
                    then.

But before that
happens,
                    it gets worse.

# SOMEONE ELSE IS BARFING TOO

A girl.

Ricki.

    And Ammiah
        right behind her.

Except … she's not saying
                BARF
but woofing out an actual
                BARK!
                        fierce and angry.

Like my own personal attack dog.

She goes at
Barf! boy.
Snarling in his face
with such intensity
I wonder if
she might actually
try to bite him.

I think he's
worried too,
because he
backs away.

*Psycho!*

he yells
at Ricki
as the bell
FINALLY
rings.

Ricki just
        laughs.

And then
howls
AWWWWWOOOOOOOO
as he turns and runs
                        away.

In that moment
I catch a bit
of Ricki's
crazy.

Her
        fearlessness,
                        too.

Throwing my arms out,
I yell
  so he
    and everyone else
                can hear—

            *You don't*
                    *mess*
                        *with the*
                            *bowling girls!*

115

# AFTER THAT

I am
part of
one of the
inside jokes.
We tell
each other
the story
again
  and
    again.

Ricki,
rabid and barking.
Ammiah,
worrying
someone will
call animal
control.

And then
      quiet
          June,
yelling out
  the line
    that becomes
      our rallying cry—

YOU DON'T MESS WITH THE
BOWLING GIRLS!

# BENNY AND I

have three
classes *and*
              lunch
together.

Last year
(after the video),
I hid in the library
during lunch.

I couldn't
stand the idea
of people
        watching
me eat.

But I don't
tell Benny
that when
we compare schedules
and he says,
*Same*
    *lunch*
        *period—*
              *Nice!*

Instead I
just answer,
*Yeah, cool.*

# MY LUNCH

is turkey
on wheat
and a
banana.

All summer
I've eaten
this every day.

I've made
        myself eat
                every bite.

I've made myself
        deal with
                the feeling
                    of food
                        FILLING
                            my belly
and staying there.

But now,
sitting
across from
Benny,
    I can't eat.

I take a bite.
Try to chew.
And can't.

The food
        is THICK
like paste,
        and I
            FIGHT
                to swallow
                    it down.

After that,
I bring
smoothies
to lunch,
usually still
half-frozen
after spending
the night
in the
freezer.

I chip away
at the drink
and
I'm pathetically
grateful
when
nobody
says
        a word
about it.

# THE WEIGHT ROOM

at school
is for
everyone
                    ... in theory.

But it
smells
like boys,
and it's full
of boys
who make it clear
this is
                        their space.

It was,
of course,
Ricki's idea
to come here.
Supposedly
to help our game,
but really
she heard
that the boys
make girls feel
unwelcome.

The others
see it as
an adventure
and a break

from the alley.
But I hate this.
All the boys.
All the eyes.
The little
snickers
as we walk by.

Ricki holds her head
high.

*Don't*
   *mind*
       *us,*

she announces loudly.
A challenge in her voice.

It's like she wants
                        a fight.

*Hey,*
  *you using this?*

Ricki asks,
nudging a boy
standing near
a machine.

The boy turns.

                        And it's Toby.

# THERE IS WEIGHT

between us.

The kind
that clanks
when it
falls.

But there's
also the
weight
of the
past.

And then
finally,
the
weight
of me.

I feel
every
pound
in this room
as I take
up space
that isn't
mine.

I grow
heavier

as
Ricki
drags us
around the room,
pushing
her way in.

I haven't
lifted a
single weight
but I'm
sweating.

It's me.
It's Toby.
It's Ricki
and all
the boys
    staring
      smirking
       stinking
        and noisy,
           too—
The weight
    of it all
      is too much.

*Bathroom*,

I gasp.
And then,
like a coward,
        I flee.

# MOM SAID

she wasn't
going to
get carried away
with wedding prep.

But she does.

First it
was just
gonna be
a backyard
thing.

But then
she and Bill
rent out
the Fire Hall.

And she
starts saying
things like,
*I saw this*
*idea on*
*Pinterest*
*for how to*
*use Mason jars*
*and tea candles*
*to make*
*centerpieces.*

Before Bill's

proposal,
Mom didn't even know
what Pinterest was.

But the thing
that's making
her craziest
                is the dress.

She found
the perfect one
early on.

It's soft
beige
with
lacey bits
around the
collar.
The "perfect length"
to show off
her legs.

It's gorgeous.

Except …
        it's one size
                too small.

Now Mom
types every
food into
her phone

before
taking a bite.

And sometimes
she says,
*Aw, the heck
with it,
I'm not
dieting
on a Friday*
(or Saturday or Sunday or whatever day it is).

Then she
makes it up
with a bunch
of laxatives
the next day.

# SHE TRIES TO HIDE IT

From me.

But mostly
        from Bill.

He says to her,
when he thinks
I won't hear,
*Maybe this*
*isn't good*
*for June?*
*Seeing you*
*worrying*
*so much*
*about weight?*

Then it
turns into
                        a fight.

Mom tells him
he doesn't know
what he's
talking about.
And if
he's gonna be
like this,
then maybe
they shouldn't
get married.

127

That's usually
when I put
my headphones on.

Weirdly, the
next day,
I'm relieved
that Bill
is still here.

Funny,
somehow
the idea
of Bill
leaving
no longer
seems like
the best thing
ever.

# WE LOSE OUR FIRST BOWLING MATCH

I expect Ricki
               to freak out.

But instead,
        she shrugs
               it off.

Says,
*It was*
*first game*
*jitters.*
*Now we've got*
*that out of*
*our system!*

I'm not
    so sure …

But clearly,
Ricki knows
better than me,
because
next match,
               we kill it.

Or Ammiah does,
and the rest of us
don't hold her back.

I'm relieved
to not be
the worst
on the team.

Laurel, Kimi,
and I are all
about the same,
score-wise.

In my case,
I tend to
get
    hot
       and
           cold
streaks.

When I'm cold,
I'll throw
gutter balls
for five frames
until I want
to run
in the bathroom
and hide.

# IT DOESN'T HELP

that Benny
is usually
at the alley,
cheering us
on.

And that
the others
are noticing
how he never
came to all their
games **before**.

Then they
laugh
and send
knowing
          looks
my way.

# LUCKILY

I haven't
      whiffed
a whole
match.

I tend to
get hot
around the
end.

Which is nice
because that
last frame
rewards
strikes and spares.

Twice I've
bowled
turkeys.
      (That's
         three strikes
           in a row).

And that,
      unfortunately,
is how
I finally
get my
bowling girls'
nickname.

# THEY CALL ME THE GOBBLER

It's because
they gobble
at me
after I bowl
the turkey.

It
    SHOULD
        be funny.

But I
hear
the word
                GOBBLE
and see
myself
   shoving
      food
        in.

I can't
tell them
I hate it.

So I just
    smile
and pretend
    to laugh
with everyone
    else.

# BENNY ASKS ME OUT

by asking
if I'm
interested
in seeing
some big
superhero
movie.

I say,
*Yeah, I guess.*

And he says,
*Well, let's go
          together.*
*Friday night?*

I've never
          been
               asked out
                    before.

I've never
          been
               on a real
                    date.

# OR MAYBE IT'S NOT A DATE

Maybe we're just friends
seeing a movie
together.

But I don't
        think so.

When I tell
Mae, she texts,

Of course
it's a date!
Don't be
a goose!

Eek!
So excited
for you!

And I
can't wait
to meet
him when
I come
for Mom's
wedding.

Only three
weeks away
now!

# JUST READING THOSE WORDS

makes
me tense up.

Mom is
getting
more and more
wedding
crazy.

But I don't
tell Mae this.

I don't want
her to
not come.

So instead,
I ask if she's
bringing her
man, too.

Again,
  I wait
   as she
    …   …   …   …

Finally,
she writes—

Maybe.

# WE'RE WINNING

more matches
than we lose.

Ammiah even
breaks a record.

Ricki says,
*We're going to*
*the girls' championship*
*for sure!*

But Polly
says,
*Realistically,*
*        we're on*
*                the bubble.*
*Other teams*
*                are undefeated.*
*And*
*next week*
***we*** *play*
*an undefeated*
*team.*

Ricki just grins.
*They won't*
*be undefeated*
*when we're*
*through with them.*

# THAT'S HOW RICKI IS

Always optimistic.

But when we
lose,
she never
gets upset.
Or points fingers.

She just sets
her steely gaze
on a distant
point
that no one else
can see,
and says,
*Next time, ladies.*
*We'll get them*
*next time.*

# HOW DO PEOPLE

go out
with someone
and act normal
even though
they like
the person
so much
that it makes
their hands
sweat?

I think about Lacey,
how she might have
some insight.
But since she traded
our friendship
for Mr. Stage Crew,
maybe she's not
the best person
to ask.
What I'd ask:
Why does
something
that's
meant to be
      fun(!)
        and
         exciting(!)
feel more
like torture?

# I ALMOST CANCEL

Say that
I'm sick.

But I
can't
because
tomorrow
is our
match
against
the undefeated
team,
and Benny
will be
there.

So I go.

# THE MOMENT I SEE BENNY

I feel better …

Because
I can tell
he's nervous,
too.

And weirdly,
it makes me feel
less alone.

# BENNY TAKES MY HAND

as we walk into
the movie theater

together,

where anyone
            and everyone
   can see
                        he is with me.

I've been invisible
I've been picked last
and left out.

I've been Toby's secret,
      the girl he liked
            but wouldn't
                be seen with.

But I've never been
                        chosen.

I lace my fingers
with Benny's,
letting him know—
                I choose him, too.

# A BUCKET OF POPCORN

                sits between

Benny                &                    me.

Greasy,
glistening
with
butter,
and
smelling
like
heaven.

I didn't eat
all day.

I was
too nervous
and I wanted
to wear
my skinny
jeans.

I eat
                    one piece—
letting it
        melt
           on my
                tongue.

143

# THE MOVIE STARTS

and I
can't help
myself—

I take a
handful.

Just    one.

Just    one.

                 MORE.

My brain
clicks off.

I forget
about calories
and Benny
beside me.

                             I just eat.

Until …

My hand
bumps
Benny's
as we
both

dig into
the bottom
of the
bucket.

*Hey,*

he nudges me
playfully.

*You're just
as bad as
Ammiah,
hogging all
the snacks.*

# MY WHOLE BODY PRICKLES

hot with
shame.

I release
the handful
of popcorn
filling my
palm.

My stomach—
      painfully
         FULL—
      pressssssssses
against
the waistband
of my jeans.

         I'm going to be sick.

# I PUSH THROUGH

the row of
people
and then
race down
the stairs.

Stomach
churning,
I hit the
door with
both hands.
SLAMMING
it open.

The bathroom
is right
in front of me,
and I want
so badly
to stand over
the toilet—

          But I can't,
             not in public.

Instead, I keep going
down the
long hallway
through the
lobby,

                    the scent
                of popcorn
                        now
                        sickening.

And out into
the parking lot.

I gulp
in air
like I've
just run
a marathon.

*June.*

It's Benny.

He must have
followed me.

I hug myself
and stare
at my feet.

*I'm so sorry,*
he says,

*I didn't mean …*
        *I should've*
                *realized …*

He sounds
upset,
his voice
shaky.

*It's okay,*
I say,
but I am
still unable
to look
at him.

Not because
I'm mad
at him,
but because
I don't
want him
to see me.

I am a
                Hog.
I am the
                Gobbler.
I'm a
                Fat Girl
                        with
                                no
                                    self-
                                        control.

149

We stand in silence
until finally Benny asks,
*Do you want
to go home, or …?*
I nod my head
while tears
pulse behind
my eyelids.

My first date.
And I ruined it.
Earlier,
    I'd worried
        over whether
            he might
                kiss me.
I'd only been
            kissed
                once before.
But now,
as we
drive in
silence,
I know
there will
be no
kiss.

And probably
no second
date either.

# BACK HOME

my
belly
    BULGES
as the
popcorn
seems to
    GROW
inside of
me.

I don't
    want
      to puke.

I want
    to be
      good.

I want
    to be
      better.

But I
can't
live with
this feeling
of fullness.

I get
a glass
of water

thinking
I'll
pee it out.

That's when
I see
Mom's
big bulk bottle
of laxatives.

I tell myself:

It's medicine.
            It's healthy.
                        It's normal.

I take three.

      And then
                        later
                                    three more.

Then I
cry myself
to sleep.

# STOMACH CRAMPS

wake me
at 5 a.m.

My stomach
is angry
as I run
to the
bathroom.

Our match
is at 10 a.m.

I need
to be
better
by then.

I can't
miss it.

Without
six players,
we forfeit.

But the
cramps
get worse
with every
hour that
passes.

# AT 9 A.M.

there's
no putting
it off
any longer.

I call
Ricki.

*I can't*
*make it*
*today,*
I tell her.
*I don't*
*feel good.*

Typical Ricki,
she wants
to know more.

*Is it a cold?*
*Can you take*
*a decongestant*
*and make it*
*through?*

I don't
want to
tell her
it's my
stomach.

I don't
     want her
          to suspect.
But she
keeps
pushing.

She wants me to call
Kimi's dad
who's a doctor
and see if he can
give me something.

Finally, I snap.
*It's one match, Ricki!*
*It's not*
*the end*
*of the*
*world.*
*It's just*
*stupid bowling.*
*And it's*
*none of your*
*business*
*what's*
*wrong*
*with me.*
*All right?*
*So just*
*leave me*
          *alone.*

And she does.

# I SKIP SCHOOL

Monday and Tuesday
pretending
to still be
sick.

But Wednesday,
Mom tells me,

*You're going.*

So I go.

# I SKIP LUNCH

avoiding Benny.

I don't
want him
finding me
in the library
either,
so I wander
the halls
killing time
until the
bell rings.

And that's
when I
run into ...
                    Toby.

# I EXPECT HIM TO PRETEND

not to
know me.

As usual.

But instead
he says,

> *June.*

Like he's
    happy to
        see
            me.

No, not
        happy.

More like …
        relieved.

He pulls
me into
the smaller
gym,
which is
    quiet and
                empty.

# MASTERS OF HIDING

That's always been
Toby and me.

But now …
he looks
different.

Smaller
somehow.

Duller.

Like some
light
in him
has flickered
out.

*June,*
he says again …

But before
he can say
more,
the door
from the
boys' locker room
opens.

Toby and I
don't need to
discuss it.

Together we
duck into the
shadows of
the bleachers,
disappearing
just as
basketballs
start
BoUnCiNg
across the floor.

Toby grimaces.

Leaning into me,
he says,
*Coach lets us*
*use this space*
*to practice*
*if we got*
*free time.*

I nod
but don't
understand
why Toby
is with
          me
instead of
              them.

# THEN HIS TEAMMATES START TALKING...

and it
      all
            becomes
                  clear.

*Dude, did
you see
Toby's mom
at the game
last night?*

The other two
laugh in a
                  nasty
sort of way.

*She was
      druuuuuunk,*
the second guy
                  adds.

*My mom said
she smelled
like a brewery.
Man, I wish
I'd seen her
fall on her face,*
another voice
comes in.
*I heard it was
HILARIOUS.*

161

*Maggie saw it.*
*She tripped*
*over **nothing,***
*and went*
*down the*
*bleachers*
*till*

       **SMACK.**

I have heard
enough,
    but they keep
        going.

How she
spat blood
in the face
of a parent
who helped
her up.

And swore at
another who
wanted to call
an ambulance.

# I LOOK AT MY SHOES

Unable to face
Toby.

Unable to
see
him
with all
his secrets
echoing
across
the gym.

# SILENCE

fills the gym
at last.

It's once again
just Toby
    and me.

I sneak
a glance
at him.

Our eyes
    meet …
        hold …

*I'm sorry about your mom,*
I say.

*Yeah,*
he answers.
*Well, it doesn't
matter anyway.
My mom's already
saying how much
she **hates** it here.
And Grans is never
coming out of
that nursing home.
So, I'll be
outta here soon.*

# HE SHRUGS LIKE IT'S NO BIG DEAL

But I can tell …
                    it's a big deal.

*You're really …*
                    *moving?*

I say,
shocked at
how much
the idea
                    *hurts.*

He shrugs again,
the movement
jerky,
like a tic
he can't
control.

*My mom*
*never likes*
*staying in*
*one place*
*too long.*

I say *sorry*
again,
feeling
stupid.

Toby gives me
one of his
old Toby
smiles—
the kind I feel
in
    my
        belly.

*It's fine,*
he says.
*New place,*
       *new secrets.*

# I GET IT

Somewhere
new.
Somewhere
no one
knows him.
Somewhere
Toby can be
          anyone.

Well,
          anyone
except
          himself.

*Aren't you
          tired?*
I ask.

          (I want to add—
          *Hiding.*
          *Pushing away*
                    *anyone who*
                              *gets close.*
          *It's exhausting.*
               *Isn't it?*)

I don't—can't—say it aloud.
But maybe
Toby hears it
anyway.

He gives me
a sad smile.

*Sometimes.*
*Yeah.*

*But what*
*else*
*can I do?*
Unexpectedly,
his hand
brushes against
mine, and then
closes around it.

*I've missed you, June,*
Toby says, softly,
these words
I wanted so badly
for so long
to hear.

*I've felt bad*
*seeing you*
*dealing with …*
*stuff.*
*Here at school.*

I swallow hard.
Knowing Toby
is talking about
BARF boy,

and the others
like him.

*They don't stop.*
*Those types—*
*they never do.*

*I wish you could*
*come with me.*
*Away.*
*We could both*
*start over.*

And then Toby
leans over
and kisses me,
a quick
press of his lips
to my cheek.

This is when
my heart
used to roll
up and down
like a yo-yo,
terrified and thrilled
all at the same time.

And it does … a bit.

But mostly,
I'm thinking
how, as long as

I'm fat,
I will always be
the girl
Toby kisses
in secret.

That wouldn't change
if we went
somewhere else.

Toby won't change.
He doesn't want to.
                                    But I do.

I am tired
        of hiding.

And I am done with being
                                    alone.

I deserve someone who holds my hand
where everyone can see.

I deserve friends loud and unafraid
to stand up for me.

I stand,
and Toby grabs
for my hand.
*Don't go yet.*

I pull away.
*I gotta go.*

*But ... just so you know,*
*sometimes the bullies*
                    *do stop.*
        *You just gotta*
                *find someone*
    *to help you*
        *BARK back.*

# BILL WAITS

at home.

He asks me
  to sit down.
  Says that the
    two of us
      gotta talk
        things out.

He tells me,
  *I know*
    *you don't*
      *like me,*
*but please*
  *hear me out.*

*I understand—*
*more than*
  *you might*
    *think—*
*about what*
  *you're going*
      *through.*

*In high school,*
*I wrestled*
*and had to*
*watch my*
*weight.*

*I'd cover
my body
with
plastic wrap
and then run
to sweat
the weight off.*

*It was
        miserable.*

*I don't want
        that for you.*

*Or your mom.*

He tells me
that they
had a big
fight the
other day
when I was
                    sick.

He dumped
Mom's laxatives
in the toilet.
And he
took her
too-small dress
and cut
it into
pieces.

He thought
Mom would
         kill him.

But she
    didn't.

She told him
he was
paying for
a new dress.

And that
     was that.

Apparently, Bill's been
online on message boards
about how to
deal with
kids with
eating disorders.

He tells me
he's found
a counselor
nearby
who he thinks
maybe can help.

Once he and Mom
are married,
his insurance
will cover it.

I guess even Mom
is on board.

And then
instead of telling—
                    he asks.

He asks if I'll go.
I start to cry.
I've been going in circles
round and round
trying to empty myself out,
  till I'm hollow,
        having purged everything
                                except
                                  the shame.
I've been battling myself
                    and
                      everyone else.
Maybe it's time
to raise the white flag.
Maybe it's time
to admit
        I need help.

Bill pulls me
into a hug.
And I let him.
And I tell him
        that yes,
            I'll go
              see the counselor.

# I GO TO BOWLING PRACTICE

for the
first time
since
I missed
our match.

It's awkward.

I say,
*I'm sorry.*

And then
I tell
them
about the
date.

                    Everything.

The popcorn.
The hog comment.
The laxatives.

Ammiah says
that Benny
didn't mention
any of this.
He only said he was
the world's
biggest idiot.

Telling the truth is
                hard
but easier
        as I
            go on.

*I hate*
*the Gobbler*
*nickname,*
I say,
forcing the
words out.

*Oh shoot,*
Ricki says,
covering
her mouth.

*I didn't*
*even think!*

The others
chime in
and agree
they can
do better.

Ammiah
jumps in
and says,
*Actually,*
*I hate my*
*nickname, too.*

*It's so much
pressure!*

We all
stare at her,
surprised.

But then …
more secrets
come out.

Laurel hates
bowling
and only
does it
for her friends.

Kimi says
the smell
of Ammiah's
hand lotion
gives her
a headache.

Polly hates
the pizza
at Ten Pin.

*We all
know that,*
Ricki says.
*You tell us
ALL the time.*

Polly nods.
*Yeah, but*
*I really,*
**really**
*hate it.*

We laugh.
We hug.
We promise
to be honest
going forward.
No more secrets.
No more hiding.

Before we
leave,
I tell Ricki,
*Check*
*your email.*
*I wrote an*
*op-ed*
*for the paper*
*and if you*
*like it—*
*you can*
*print it.*

She squeals
and squeezes me
in a big hug.
Which, I'm
pretty sure
means I'm forgiven.

# TOBY IS GONE

A big FOR SALE
sign
went up.

He sent me
a text
as the U-Haul
pulled away.

> You're the only
> thing I'll miss
> round here.

I stared at it
a long time,
feeling sad
for the
first boy
I ever kissed.

Then I
wished him
good luck
and put
my phone
away.

# A SECOND CHANCE

at a first date.

Benny and I
have a do-over date.
We go
roller-skating,
a thing
we are both
very bad at.

We help
each other
fall down
and get back up.

I laugh
so much
my face hurts.

And …
at the end of the date
when he doesn't kiss me—
I make the move
and kiss *him* instead.

181

# SURPRISE

Mae comes home
the day before the wedding,
date in tow.

Thing is,
Mae's date is
not the
type of boy
I imagined
her with.

Actually,
she's
not a
boy at all.

Mae has
    a girlfriend.

I can tell
Mae is
nervous
introducing
her.

I give them
both
    big
        hugs.

Bill does, too.

Mom rolls
her eyes
and says,
*Of course
you go to
an artsy school
and come home
a lesbian.*

But then
she laughs
and hugs
them both
as well.

# THE WEDDING

is beautiful.

Mom finds
a dress
that's
hot pink,
and it fits her
               perfectly.

Mae makes
matching
soft pink
dresses for
the two of us.

Side by side
in front of
the mirror,
I am pretty sure
that we all look
               beautiful.

And I'm pretty sure
the bond between us
might be beaten up—
but it's not broken.
 Maybe now—
     it's actually even
               stronger than before.

184

# BEFORE MAE LEAVES

to go back
to school,
I show
her my
op-ed
that Ricki
printed.

I watch
her face
as she reads
the words,
that for
so long
I couldn't
say.

And when
she's done,
I finally
tell her,
*I'm sorry.*

We hug.

Mae says
　she missed me
　　　　　so much
but was too homesick
　to say it
　　　or even type it.

185

She was also
   worried
      that maybe
         I was
            better off
                  without her.

I promise her
 this will
   NEVER
   EVER
      be true.

And then
 we hug
    again—
         even harder.

# WHAT DID I WRITE

in that op-ed?

Just the truth.

Not Erick's truth
that he stole
from me.

But **my** truth.
I took it back
            from him.
And now
        I own it.

I am a fat girl
    with an eating disorder.

I used those
 two words
   that I still
            hate
because they're the
                    truth.

Which maybe
   in a way …
    *did*
     set me
        FREE.

# I'M NOT HIDING ANYMORE

And I'm
                not pretending
everything
       is
         Fine.

I'm not pushing everyone away,
  but instead
     opening up
  to my friends
    and my new psychologist
      and even Bill.  (Crazy, right?)

Because I now know
      I can't fix this
                           alone.

Do I look in the mirror
     and love myself?
            Ha.
             No.
               Not yet.

BUT …

# THE OTHER DAY

Ammiah had a photo of the bowling girls
        that I thought was from last season
            before I joined.
And I saw all these gorgeous confident girls
        with big goofy grins,
            cheesing at the camera.

Then, I realized one of them was me.
It was a photo from this season.
**I** was one of those gorgeous girls.

        How about that?

# LATELY I FEEL LIGHTER

even as I'm
            taking
                    up
                            more
                                    space.

And I think
        maybe,
                just maybe,
    *this*
is how it's
supposed
    to feel
when
    I'm honest
        and open
            and brave enough
                    to try and be—
                        all of me.

Always June.

# WANT TO KEEP READING?

If you liked this book, check out another book
from West 44 Books:

## *CATCH ME IF I FALL*
## BY CLAUDIA RECINOS SELDEEN

ISBN: 9781978596351

# BALANCING ACT

*Hang*
*on*
*tight!*

When I'm on a trapeze,
I defy gravity.

I'm a leaf
caught in a summer storm.
Twisting.
Spinning.

But there's always that voice
in the back of my mind,
whispering:

*Hang*
*on*
*tight.*

*Don't*
*let*
*go.*

*Falling is not an option.*

# DANCE TRAPEZE

When I tell people
I'm a
trapeze artist,
their eyes
light up
like stars.

I know
they're thinking about
flying
        trapeze.
About acrobats
w h i z z i n g
through the air.

But
dance
        trapeze
is
different.

There's no
swinging.
No catching.
No letting go.

A
dance
        trapeze
doesn't
tick tock
back and forth.

A
dance
          trapeze
spins
in tight circles.

It twirls
and turns.

If you don't hold on,
it will
spin
you
right
off.

**CHECK OUT MORE BOOKS AT:**

www.west44books.com

# ABOUT THE AUTHOR

Kate Karyus Quinn is an avid reader and menthol chapstick addict. She lives in the suburbs of Buffalo, New York, with her husband, three children, and two dogs. She is the author of several books, including: *Anti/Hero*, a middle grade graphic novel with DC Comics, and *Not Hungry*, a book in verse that was a Junior Library Guild selection.